A catalogue record for this book is available from the British Library

Published by Ladybird Books Ltd Loughborough Leicestershire UK
Ladybird Books Ltd is a subsidiary of the Penguin Group of companies
LADYBIRD and the device of a Ladybird are trademarks of Ladybird Books Ltd

© The Walt Disney Company MCMXCVI
Printed in Belgium

Deep in the forest, a new day was beginning. Spring had come at last, and bright new leaves were sprouting everywhere. All the animals and birds were waking up and getting ready for the day ahead. All, that is, except Owl, who had spent the night hunting and was now feeling *very* tired. He hardly noticed the squirrel stretching and yawning loudly on the branch above.

Feeling hungry, the squirrel climbed down the tree to go in search of some breakfast.

"Hello, Miss Mouse," she said to a little mouse who was scurrying by. "Did you know it's springtime again?"

"Yes, it's lovely, isn't it!" Miss Mouse replied with a happy smile on her face.

Suddenly, they heard the sound of running and a group of animals and birds burst through the undergrowth.

Thumper the rabbit was leading the way. "It's happened!" he called.

The commotion woke Owl. He blinked his eyes and shouted crossly, "What's going on?"

"Wake up!" called Thumper, pounding his foot in delight. "The new Prince is born. We're all going to see him!" And he dashed off to join the others.

Owl fluffed out his feathers and followed.

As soon as they reached the thicket, everyone crept forward very quietly to get a clear view of the new Prince.

There, in the shade of a tree, lay Mother Deer with a tiny fawn asleep at her side.

One by one, the animals stepped forward to congratulate her and to admire the little Prince.

"Thank you very much!" said Mother Deer, looking around at everyone. Then gently nuzzling the small head beside her, she whispered, "Come on... wake up! We have company."

The fawn opened his eyes, blinked, then yawned. He seemed very confused and a little frightened.

Thumper hopped closer to them. "Hello, little Prince," he said. Then he looked up at Mother Deer. "What are you going to call him?" he asked.

"Well... I think I'll call him Bambi," she said.

"This is quite an occasion!" Owl hooted. "It isn't every day a prince is born. But it looks to me as if he's getting very sleepy. I think it's time we all left." And everyone slowly moved away.

Thumper could hardly wait for the new Prince to wake up so that they could play together. The little rabbit returned later that day to watch Bambi take his first wobbly steps. "He doesn't walk very well, does he?" cried Thumper, who was swiftly warned by his mother to be quiet.

But he didn't have to stay quiet for very long. Soon his new friend Bambi wanted to explore the forest, and Thumper was keen to show him the way.

Bambi found that his new world was full of surprises. Clambering over the tree roots and through the thick undergrowth, he soon discovered he had many new friends.

"Good morning, young Prince!" shouted Mrs Quail and her family.

"Good morning, young Prince!" cried another voice above Bambi's head. He looked up and was amazed to see a mother and three baby opossums, hanging by their tails from a branch.

"How strange," he thought. Bambi bent over to see how things looked upside down, but he soon gave up. He was getting quite dizzy.

Thumper taught Bambi his very first word. It happened one day when they were exploring the forest. Suddenly, a bird flew overhead.

"That's a *bird*," said Thumper.

"Bird!" repeated Bambi.

Then a butterfly landed on Bambi's tail. "Bird?" he said.

"No, no," laughed Thumper. "That's a butterfly."

"Butterfly," said Bambi, shaking his tail.

The butterfly flew off to rest on a nearby flower.

"Butterfly?" said Bambi.

"No, that's a flower," corrected Thumper.

Bambi bent down to sniff the pretty, sweet-scented blooms in front of him. Suddenly, he found that he was nose to nose with another creature, whose big friendly eyes were staring up at him.

"Flower!" announced Bambi.

"Who, me?" queried the skunk, looking surprised.

"No, no, no…" laughed Thumper, rolling on the ground kicking his big paws in delight. "That's not a *flower*… he's a little skunk."

"Oh, that's all right," giggled the skunk bashfully. "He can call me a flower if he wants to!"

And the three friends went off to explore the forest together.

24

One day, when he was lying sleepily with his mother in the thicket, Bambi awoke to the sound of dripping. He watched as little drops of water fell on the leaves all around.

Bambi's mother explained to him that it was raining. "All the leaves will become greener and new flowers will grow and bloom," she said.

Soon the little April shower turned into quite a heavy rainstorm. Bambi watched as each of the forest animals scampered about trying to find shelter.

A mother bird spread out her wings like a large umbrella to keep her newborn babies dry and warm. One of the little birds popped its head out for a second… and quickly hid again as the raindrops landed on his head.

When Bambi was old enough, his mother led him through the forest to the meadow.

"What's a meadow?" asked Bambi, skipping beside her.

"It's a very wonderful and dangerous place," said his mother. "Now remember! You must always stay where I can find you, and come when I call."

The meadow looked like a huge carpet full of flowers. Bambi gazed in wonder at the great new world before him. Suddenly he spotted Thumper and soon felt at home. He realised that many of his forest friends had come to the meadow, too.

He leapt over the grass and flowers towards them. "What are you eating?" Bambi asked the rabbits in front of him.

"Clover... it's really tasty!" said Mrs Rabbit.

"It's delicious!" agreed Thumper. "Why don't you try some, Bambi?" The little rabbit quickly ducked his head among the flowers. He opened his mouth and was just about to take a large mouthful of blossom, when his mother called.

"Thumper! What did your father tell you about eating blossoms and leaving the greens?"

Thumper reluctantly recited the rhyme his father had taught him:

"Eating greens is a special treat.
It makes long ears and great big feet!"

He pulled a face at Bambi and, leaning close so that his mother couldn't hear, he whispered a line that he had added himself, *"But it really isn't nice to eat!"* Bambi grinned and they skipped away through the grassy meadow.

Bambi and Thumper stopped to rest beside a pool of water. Suddenly a large frog hopped out from among the reeds and landed on a rock. Bambi looked up in surprise.

"Watch out!" croaked the frog and leapt back into the water.

"That's a frog," said Thumper, sounding very wise. "When we've gone it will pop its head out of the water again and play hide-and-seek with the other frogs."

Bambi smiled, and moved closer to the water's edge to take a drink. Bending over, he saw another fawn exactly like him looking back. He hesitated for a moment. "That's your reflection," explained Thumper.

Suddenly, Bambi heard the sound of someone giggling close by. He raised his head and found himself staring into the eyes of another fawn.

The other fawn giggled and skipped around him, trying to get him to play. But Bambi was uncertain and backed away… straight into the pond!

The other little fawn licked his cheek and ran away. Bambi got up to follow and found her near to his mother and another doe.

"This is little Faline, your cousin," his mother explained. "And this is your aunt. Aren't you going to say hello?"

Soon Bambi and Faline became good friends. They started chasing round their mothers' legs and laughing loudly.

Suddenly they realised that all the animals had become very quiet. They followed their gaze towards the forest.

Bambi watched in awe as a large stag walked proudly towards him. The stag inspected Bambi and then continued majestically back to the forest.

"Why did everyone stop when the stag came?" he asked his mother when the stag had gone.

"Everyone respects him," his mother replied. "For of all the deer in the forest, he is the most brave. And he's very wise… that is why he's known as the great Prince of the Forest." Then she added proudly, "And *you* are his son."

Suddenly a gun-shot rang out through the trees. All the animals and birds scattered in terror. Bambi panicked and was caught up in the rush as everyone hurried back to the forest. He didn't know what was happening, but felt he was in great danger.

Bambi dodged between the other animals. He could see Faline and his aunt a long way ahead, but there was no sign of his mother.

He searched frantically through the tall meadow grass. More shots echoed all around him.

Suddenly a large shadow appeared at his side.

The Prince looked down at Bambi. "Follow me!" he ordered and headed towards the trees. Bambi ran after him as quickly as he could. They did not stop running until they came to the densely covered thicket where the deer could safely hide.

Bambi was very pleased to see his mother again. He had not known she had been running with them, too.

Bambi cowered in terror and did not notice the great stag slip away. His mother cautiously poked her head out of the thicket to check that it was safe. "Come on, Bambi," she said. "We don't have to hide any longer."

"Why did we all run?" Bambi asked.

His mother looked down at him. "Man was in the forest," was all she said.

Soon summer was over and the passing days grew darker and colder. Winter came, and Bambi awoke one morning to find the forest completely covered in a clean white blanket.

The young Prince carefully put one hoof onto the snow to test the crisp surface. Then he stepped forward, leaving a trail of prints behind him. "This is a great game!" he thought. He looked up and saw Thumper in the distance, skating across the icy covering on the pond.

Bambi soon learnt that walking on the ice was not as simple as it looked. He skidded at once and fell heavily on his stomach. Thumper laughed and laughed, but soon came to help his friend up again.

45

When Bambi and Thumper had finished skating they went to explore the snow-covered forest. They could hear snoring coming from a little opening to a cave and peered in to see who was there. It was Flower!

They tried to get him up, but the skunk said that he would sleep until spring came. Bambi and Thumper left him to hibernate in peace.

Winter was fun at first, but as time went on, there was less and less food to eat. All the animals became hungry. Even the squirrel finished her huge store of nuts.

Bambi's mother taught him how to dig in the ground to look for plants or grass, and she tore off pieces of tree bark for him when he could not reach high enough up the trees.

The days were short and it was now very cold. But Bambi always knew he could hurry back to his mother to get warm again.

One terrible day Bambi and his mother went to the meadow to look for food. Suddenly, gun-shots rang out. Bambi's mother ordered him to run to the thicket and not look back. When he reached safety he stopped, his heart pounding. Everything was completely silent and he was alone. He looked all around, and began to call desperately for his mother...

Silently, the Prince of the Forest appeared at Bambi's side. "Your mother can't be with you any more," he said. "Man has taken her away. Now you must be brave and learn to walk alone. Come, my son."

Bambi glanced sadly back at the meadow. Then he turned to follow the great stag, knowing that he could trust him.

At last, winter was over. It was a beautiful spring day.
Cheerful love-songs filled the forest, as pairs of birds
began to build their nests. All around there seemed to be
a buzz of activity, as the forest came back to life after its
long sleep.

The spring sun shone on Prince Bambi's coat as he walked along the forest paths. He carried his head proudly, for now he had a fine set of antlers.

Flower, too, had grown big and strong. Together the two friends went in search of Thumper.

They found him talking to Owl, who was complaining bitterly about all the noise in the forest. "It's the same thing every spring," he groaned.

A pair of birds circled Owl, fluttering and twittering. "Stop that racket!" he roared.

"What's the matter with them?" asked Flower.

"Don't you know?" asked Owl. The three friends shook their heads. "They're twitterpated!" cried Owl.

Flower, Thumper and Bambi looked bewildered. "*Twitterpated*?" they said.

"Nearly everyone gets twitterpated in spring," Owl explained. "They see a pretty face – and suddenly they're in love. And love can make you quite crazy. It can also make you sing a lot, which is why owls like me don't get any sleep at this time of the year!"

"That sounds awful!" said Thumper.

"Be careful, my friends," warned Owl. "It could happen to you!"

The three friends shook their heads in disgust. "Never," they vowed.

But their wise friend Owl was absolutely right! That very same day, Bambi watched as first Flower, then Thumper, fell in love.

So the young Prince set out by himself for a walk in the forest. He stopped by a pool to get a drink, and suddenly saw the reflection of a beautiful doe in the water.

"Don't you remember me?" asked the doe smiling. "I'm Faline!"

Bambi backed away clumsily and caught his antlers in the blossom above. He shook his head, first to try to free himself, and then as Faline licked him on the cheek.

All at once Bambi felt extremely happy. Like Flower and Thumper before him, he was falling in love.

Bambi and Faline set off together down the forest path.

"Not so fast," said a deep voice. "Faline is going with me." The path of Bambi was blocked by the sharp antlers of a jealous buck. Bambi did not want to fight, but he realised that he had no choice.

The buck moved across to Faline and pushed her to one side.

"Bambi!" she cried out fearfully.

The young Prince swayed his head from side to side in anger. He pawed the ground, then lowered his head and charged at the buck.

The two deer clashed fiercely, their antlers locked together. Bambi backed the buck against a tree, but suddenly lost his footing and was tossed to the ground. He quickly leapt up and ran straight at his enemy once more. Their antlers clashed together with a loud crack, and both deer retreated. Bambi climbed up onto a rock and lowered his head to charge. The buck reared up on its hind legs and kicked out as Bambi approached.

Bambi prepared to charge for the third time. Faline could hardly bear to watch as the two deer balanced precariously on the edge of a cliff.

With a toss of his head, Bambi knocked his opponent to one side. He watched the buck slide over the cliff side and land in the water below.

Knowing he was beaten, the buck limped away back into the forest.

Faline came to Bambi's side and proudly kissed him. There was nothing to fear any more.

The months passed by and soon it was autumn.

One morning Bambi woke early. He sensed danger all around and leaving Faline asleep, he went to find his father. They went to the hill top and saw smoke coming from a large campfire.

"It's Man," said the great stag. "He is here again. There are many this time. We must go deep into the forest... hurry! Follow me!"

The terrible news spread quickly through the forest. All the animals scurried about in fright, uncertain whether to flee or find somewhere to hide near their homes.

Thumper gathered his large family together and pointed them towards a deep hidden burrow.

Meanwhile, Bambi left the great stag and headed back towards the thicket in search of Faline. He could hear fierce dogs barking near to where he had left her that morning.

He turned the corner and saw to his horror that Faline was trapped on a ledge with a huge pack of dogs jumping up at her. Bambi charged forwards scattering the pack and giving Faline the seconds she needed to escape.

The dogs regrouped and, snarling ferociously, they rushed together against Bambi.

The young Prince swiftly took to his heels and fled across the rocks. The dogs continued to race after Bambi, until he reached a gorge. Bambi kicked out his powerful hind legs and pushed himself into the air. Suddenly a shot rang out, and Bambi felt a sharp, stinging pain in his shoulder. He stiffened and fell to the ground.

Bambi wanted to rest, but a voice he knew well ordered him to get up. "The forest is in great danger, Bambi. You must get up, *at once!*"

Making a tremendous effort, Bambi rose to his feet and limped away after his father. He saw that the forest was filled with smoke. Huge flames flared up around them, engulfing the trees. The fire, which had started at the campsite, swept quickly through the dry fallen leaves.

Fear outweighed the pain in Bambi's shoulder, as he kept up with his father. They dived this way, then that, through the burning forest. At last they came to the river and leapt into the water so that they could swim to safety.

Bambi and Faline were reunited on an island in the middle of the river. All the other birds and animals had made their way there, too. They watched in silence as their home was engulfed in flames, and burnt out to a charred, black mass.

The squirrel yawned
and stretched. She wanted
to jump and somersault in
the trees after her long
winter's sleep. Just as she
was getting ready to leap,
Thumper the rabbit
arrived. "Have you heard
the news?" he asked,
pounding his foot on the
ground.

The noise woke Owl, who was dozing in the tree above. "Oh… what now?" he asked grumpily.

"It's happened! It's happened!" shouted several happy voices, as they gathered round the tree.

Thumper had already announced the good news to the other animals. They rushed in from every corner of the forest and made their way towards the thicket.

As they drew closer to the place where Bambi and Faline lived, the animals lowered their voices.

"Shh," whispered Thumper. "Be quiet, or you may wake them. Look... over there!"

The new-born Prince and Princess of the Forest were resting in the thicket, as their father had done once, a long time ago.

"Well, sir..." said Owl, "I don't believe I've ever seen a more likely looking pair of fawns! Prince Bambi ought to be extremely proud."

The animals raised their heads and looked across to the hillside. There stood Bambi and his father majestically watching over them.

Bambi turned to bid his father a last fond farewell. The old Prince went deep into the woodland to take his final rest.

Bambi strode back down the hillside to Faline and the fawns. The forest had a new prince now and Bambi was determined to rule as wisely and bravely as his father before him.

The forest, and all the animals who lived there, would be safe in his care.